Lulu Bell and the

Birthday Unicorn

A Random House book
Published by Random House Australia Pty Ltd
Level 3, 100 Pacific Highway, North Sydney NSW 2060
www.randomhouse.com.au

First published by Random House Australia in 2013

Addresses for companies within the Random House Group can be found at
www.randomhouse.com.au/offices

National Library of Australia
Cataloguing-in-Publication Entry

Author: Murrell, Belinda
Title: Lulu Bell and the birthday unicorn/Belinda Murrell; Serena Geddes, illustrator
ISBN: 978 1 74275 875 6 (pbk.)
Series: Murrell, Belinda. Lulu Bell; 1
Target audience: For primary school age
Subjects: Ponies – Juvenile fiction
          Birthday parties – Juvenile fiction
          Children's stories
Other authors/contributors: Geddes, Serena
Dewey number: A823.4

Cover and internal illustrations by Serena Geddes
Cover design by Christabella Designs
Internal design and typesetting in 16/22 pt Bembo by Anna Warren, Warren Ventures
Printed in Australia by Griffin Press, an accredited ISO AS/NZS 14001:2004
Environmental Management System printer

Lulu Bell and the Birthday Unicorn

Belinda Murrell

Illustrated by Serena Geddes

RANDOM HOUSE AUSTRALIA

Molly   Lulu   Dad

Mum   Gus   Rosie

For my mum and dad, who gave me the best possible childhood growing up in a vet hospital. My memories are filled with loving family and friends, exciting adventures and animals, and of course books.

Chapter 1

The Cake

Lulu and her best friend, Molly, were in the kitchen, helping Lulu's mum. Lulu was adding the final decoration to a mermaid birthday cake, and Molly was spooning chocolate crackle mixture into patty cases.

'Do you think the mermaid needs another pearl in her hair?' asked Lulu.

On a large wooden board was the most beautiful cake Lulu had ever seen.

It was a mermaid with long curly
hair made of spun sugar. Her tail was
a silvery-green that shimmered and
sparkled. She swam upon a sea of
crunchy blue lollies. All around her were
golden fish and shells.

Lulu's mum was an artist. She had

2

spent hours sculpting the mermaid body and mixing the icing. Lulu had helped to choose the colours. It was just the right cake for her little sister Rosie's sixth birthday party.

'Three pearls looks perfect,' said Lulu's mum. 'Rosie will love it.'

At their feet was Jessie, the smiliest dog in the world. Her long pink tongue lolled out and she thumped her tail on the floor.

'It looks way too good to eat,' agreed Molly. 'You should take a photo of it.'

The girls admired the cake while Mum snapped some photographs. Jessie snuffled around and licked up specks of green icing from the floor. Pickles, one of the family cats, stalked into the kitchen. She hissed at the big brown dog and chased her away.

3

Over in the corner, curled in her basket, was another dog: Jessie's mother, Asha. She was grey around her muzzle and much quieter than her daughter. She lifted one ear and watched everyone with alert brown eyes.

'Great, that's done,' said Mum. 'We'll leave it on the bench for the icing to set. Now, we still have to finish the chocolate crackles, make the blue jelly and bake a big batch of brownies. *And* make sure Gus doesn't stick his fingers into anything.'

A loud shout came from the back garden. The door banged open. A tiny superhero ran through the doorway and skidded to a halt right by the table. A pair of brown eyes gleamed through a black mask. They stared straight at the chocolate crackles.

'Hello, honey bun,' said Mum.

'Are you having fun?'

'I not honey bun,' insisted Gus.
'I Bug Boy.'

Gus was wearing a red-and-green superhero outfit that Mum had made. It had a long green cloak and green leggings. Gus loved it so much that he refused to take it off – even when he was having a bath.

'Isn't he adorable?' cooed Mum.

Lulu glanced at her friend and raised her eyebrows. Molly giggled. Lulu loved her younger brother and sister. But sometimes their antics could be a little annoying. She prided herself on being the practical one in the family.

'I not *'dorable* – I Bug Boy,' Gus shouted. He grabbed a chocolate crackle from the plate and ran off. Jessie chased at his heels.

'Gus,' Lulu yelled after him, her hands on her hips. 'That's for Rosie's party.'

Gus, of course, didn't reply. Mum smiled lovingly and kept mixing the brownie batter.

The door to the lounge room swung open. It revealed Rosie. A cloud of fine

dark hair framed her face. She wore a
white dress, sparkly silver thongs and a
pair of feathery angel wings. She was
using both hands to carry a big basket of
pencils, pastels and paints.

'I'm going to start decorating the
lolly bags,' announced Rosie.

'Look, Rosie,' called Lulu. 'We've

finished the mermaid
cake. It looks amazing.'

'Oooooh,' squealed
Rosie. She leaned over
the platter. 'She's beautiful, Mum,
thank you. That is the best cake I have
ever seen.'

Mum kissed the top of Rosie's head.
'A pleasure, honey bun. The lolly bags are
on the table.'

Asha came to lie under the kitchen
table to keep Rosie company.

Next, Lulu and Molly made
turquoise-blue jelly. Mum poured boiling

water onto the jelly crystals in the jug and stirred. The girls added the cold water and took their turns to stir. They carefully poured the liquid into sixteen small plastic cups.

'We have to wait until the jelly is half-set. Then we can decorate each cup with green snakes to look like seaweed,' explained Lulu. 'Mum thinks it will look really pretty.'

'It will taste yummy, too,' agreed Molly. She licked a drop of mixture from her finger.

The girls had just slid the tray of jelly cups into the fridge when the phone rang. Mum switched off the mixer and answered it.

'Hello, Shelly Beach Vet, Chrissie speaking.'

She paused, listening to the caller.

Lulu's dad was a veterinary surgeon, and their house was right behind the vet hospital. When Kylie, the vet nurse, was busy with patients, the phone rang through to the house.

'Mmmm, I see . . . I'll tell Dr Bell . . . Yes, he'll be there as soon as possible . . .'

Mum hung up, frowning.

'Honey bun, could you please give your dad a message? A pony is running loose on the Parkway,' said Mum. 'It's a busy road and the pony could be hit by a car. We need to send someone up to catch it right away.'

'A pony?' asked Lulu. Her face creased with concern. She had always loved horses and the thought of one in danger worried her. 'Dad might need some help with it.'

Mum nodded.

'Just remind Dad that it's Rosie's mermaid party this afternoon. We'll have ten excited six-year-olds arriving in less than three hours,' continued Mum. 'You can go with Dad, but remember I still need your help to make the lolly bags and set up all the games.'

Lulu tucked one of her honey-coloured plaits behind her ear.

'Don't worry, Mum,' said Lulu. 'Molly and I can do that when we get back.'

Chapter 2

Shelly Beach Vet Hospital

A thick green door separated the vet hospital from the house. When Lulu and Molly closed the door behind them, the familiar smell of the hospital surrounded them – a mixture of disinfectant and animal fur. Lulu loved being here. There were always lots of beautiful animals to talk to.

At the front of the vet hospital, closest to the street, was a big waiting room.

It had a counter, a huge fish tank filled with tropical fish, and shelves of pet products. Behind that were two consulting rooms where Lulu's dad saw his patients. Then there was the hospital ward full of cages for the overnight patients. At the very back were an operating theatre, a store room and a tiny X-ray room.

Kylie, the vet nurse, appeared in the hallway. She was carrying a large fluffy cat in a carry cage. She smiled at Lulu.

'Your dad's seeing a patient in there.' Kylie pointed to one of the consulting rooms. 'He won't be long.'

'It's an emergency,' explained Lulu. 'We need to save a pony.'

'Go on in then,' said Kylie.

Dr Bell's patient was a pug with a squashed-in face and a curly tail. It yapped furiously as Lulu tapped on the

door. Its owner was an elderly lady. She
cooed and stroked the dog. With her big
fluffy coat and her own button nose, the
lady looked a lot like her pet.

14

'There, there, Iggy,' said the lady. 'The noisy little girls won't hurt you.'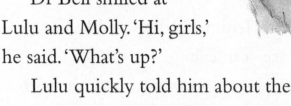

Dr Bell smiled at Lulu and Molly. 'Hi, girls,' he said. 'What's up?'

Lulu quickly told him about the escaped pony. Dr Bell frowned and nodded.

'Okay, sweetie,' he said. 'I'll just be a couple more minutes with Iggy. Why don't you fill a bucket with feed and fetch a halter and lead, then we'll go.'

Lulu led the way to the crowded store room.

The walls were lined with shelves right to the ceiling. On the floor were big bins of food for every kind of pet you could imagine. On a side table, under a heat lamp, was a closed cardboard box.

Lulu carefully opened the lid. Inside was an orphaned baby brush-tailed possum. She was curled up asleep in a nest of soft flannel.

'Hello, Jemima,' whispered Lulu. 'How are you feeling?'

The possum looked up at Lulu with round brown eyes. Her black whiskers twitched. She scampered over to Lulu and climbed onto the palm of the girl's hand. The long fluffy tail curled around Lulu's arm and tickled her bare skin.

'No, it's not milk time yet, you greedy guts,' said Lulu. She stroked the possum's back. 'I only fed you an hour ago!'

16

'I think she's grown again overnight!' said Molly. 'She is *so* cute!'

Lulu gently returned the baby to her nest. She tucked the sheet around the body to make a little pouch.

'Dad thinks she's going to be all right,' said Lulu. 'Mum gets up during the night to feed her. And Kylie or I give her a syringe of special milk every two hours during the day.'

Lulu closed the box and checked to make sure the lid was secure.

'Dad says possums are amazing escape artists,' explained Lulu. 'Once we had a possum that found his way into the kitchen. He took one bite out of every piece of fruit in the fruit bowl. Mum said it was obviously time for him to return to the wild.'

Molly laughed. 'You're so lucky, Lulu.

17

I wish we had had lots of pets. Mum will only let me have a goldfish.'

Her friend grinned. 'You can share ours.'

Lulu filled a bucket with grain pellets. Then she grabbed a halter and lead rope from the hook behind the door.

'All right, Molly,' said Lulu. She hefted the feed bucket. 'Do you want to come with us?'

'I wouldn't miss it for the world!'

Chapter 3

The Runaway

Outside, it was a warm, sunny day and
the sky was a deep blue. A soft breeze
from the east brought the tang of salt.
Lulu could hear the low rumble of the
nearby ocean. The vet hospital was just
up the hill from busy Shelly Beach. The
beach would be crowded with swimmers
and surfers on such a glorious day.

Dr Bell hitched up a high-sided
trailer behind his station wagon and they

set off. Of course, Jessie and Asha could
never miss out on a car ride. The two
dogs sat in the very back, smiling happily.

It was only a ten-minute drive to
the Parkway, where the runaway pony
had been seen. Lulu and Molly caught
glimpses of the city and the blue of
the harbour in the distance. Soon the

20

view was swallowed up by thick green bushland.

On the long straight Parkway, Dr Bell drove slowly and carefully. He glanced through the gum trees on either side.

'Keep a really good look out,' he told the girls. 'The pony may have run into the bush. At least it will be safer there.'

But the runaway had not sought the shelter of the bush.

'Look, Dad,' yelled Lulu. She pointed her finger straight ahead.

A pure white pony was galloping down the centre of the road, its tail and mane flying.

The car in front braked suddenly and its tyres screeched. It swerved to the side of the road. The driver honked the horn and frightened the runaway pony even more.

Dr Bell turned on the station wagon's hazard lights. He stopped the car and trailer so they blocked most of the road.

'That should stop any other cars coming near me or the pony!' he said. 'Now, I want you girls to stay in the car until I tell you it's safe to come out.'

Dr Bell took the bucket, halter and lead and stepped calmly and carefully into the middle of the road. He held out his hand towards the pony. Lulu and Molly watched through the open window.

The pony reared and tossed its head. It began to gallop again, heading straight towards Dr Bell. Its hooves thundered on the bitumen.

'Oh,' gasped Molly. She clutched Lulu's arm. 'Your dad's going to be run over.'

'Shhhh,' whispered Lulu. 'Dad knows what he's doing.'

'Come on, boy,' called Dr Bell gently. 'There's a good boy. Come on.'

Dr Bell stepped slowly towards the rushing pony. Its ears flicked back and forth.

'That's a good boy,' repeated Dr Bell. 'Come and have some feed.'

The pony reared and bucked, then skittered to a stop. Its sides heaved. Its neck was slick with sweat and its mane was matted with twigs and leaves. The pony paused and sniffed. Then with a huge *hurrumph*, it stepped forward and slid its head under Dr Bell's arm.

'Gooooood boy.'

Dr Bell stroked the pony's nose. He slid the lead around the pony's neck. Then he softly fastened the halter around

the pony's head.

'Come over slowly, girls,' suggested Dr Bell. 'He's still very skittery.'

Lulu and Molly climbed out of the car, leaving the dogs safely shut in the back.

'Isn't he gorgeous?' murmured Lulu.

She ran her fingers through the pony's tangled forelock. The pony was completely white, except for his dainty black hooves. His liquid brown eyes were framed with long lashes. Lulu breathed in his warm scent of hay and horse and sweat.

'I wonder who he belongs to? They must be really worried about him,' Lulu said.

She held the bucket while the pony dipped his head in. He sniffed, blew and lipped some grain.

'What are we going to do with him?' asked Molly.

Dr Bell checked the pony for injury. He ran his hands expertly down the pony's flanks and fetlocks.

'We'll take him back with us,' he replied. 'He can stay in the back garden for now. I'll phone the police and they should find his family quite quickly.'

'But Dad,' objected Lulu, 'what about Rosie's birthday party?'

Dr Bell stood up and grinned at the girls.

'Oh, he'll be no trouble,' he said. 'Rosie will love having a pony in the backyard for her party.'

By this time the Parkway was filled with stopped cars. The people closest waved and cheered as Dr Bell loaded the pony onto the trailer. The girls clambered back into the car. Jessie and Asha were overjoyed to see them again. They took turns to lick the two girls on the fingers.

'What do you think, Jess?' Lulu asked the large brown dog. 'A pony for the party?'

'Woof,' replied Jess with a smile. Asha barked in agreement.

'What if your dad can't find the owner?' asked Molly.

A grin of pure joy spread across Lulu's face. 'Then we'll have to keep him. Won't we, Dad?' she begged. 'I could ride him to school!'

'Now, don't get too excited, Lulu,' warned Dad. 'That pony looks very well cared for to me. Someone will be searching for him.'

Lulu pulled the corners of her mouth down and pouted her lips to make an extra-sad face.

'Fingers crossed,' she whispered to Molly.

Dr Bell turned the car and headed for home.

Chapter 4

Home Again

Back at the vet hospital, Dr Bell unloaded the pony from the trailer. He led him through the side gate and into the back garden. Lulu, Molly and the two dogs followed close behind.

Mum was tying bunches of green and purple balloons to the frangipani tree. Gus was chasing a flyaway balloon around the lawn. He was making a shrieking noise, like an overheated helicopter.

Jessie bounded over and joined in the game, barking madly.

'Good, you found the pony,' said Mum. 'Is he all right?'

Dr Bell locked the gate, then undid the pony's lead.

'Yes,' he replied. 'Just frightened. Gussie, you might want to quieten down a little. We don't want to alarm the pony all over again.'

'I not Gussie, I Bug Boy,' replied Gus as he zoomed past.

Lulu crossed her arms and frowned.

'Gus,' she said, 'you'll scare the pony.'

Mum smiled at Gus. 'Come inside, honey bun,' she coaxed. 'You can help the girls make the lolly bags. I'm going to decorate the front hall. And Lulu – you and Molly should get dressed. All the guests will be here in an hour.'

Dad reached up into the branches. He secured a coloured streamer that had come loose.

'I have to get back to work,' he said. 'Lots of patients will be waiting for me. Plus, I need to phone the police so they can track down the owner of this pony.'

He started walking towards the house, then turned and smiled.

'I'll come back and join the party later on,' he promised. 'You don't expect me to dress up as a merman, do you?'

Lulu grinned at the thought of her tall, gangly dad dressed as a merman.

'Of course I do,' joked Mum.

'Rosie and I have made you a perfect outfit. You will be King Neptune, Lord of the Sea.'

'*Hmph*,' grumbled Dr Bell. He pulled a silly face. 'Did I mention that I have lots of animals to see? I may not be back before dinner time.'

Everyone laughed.

Lulu, Molly and Mum headed into

the house. Rosie was sitting at the kitchen table. She was drawing pictures of mermaids on brown paper bags. Her tongue poked out of her mouth as she concentrated. Mints, chocolate frogs, jelly babies and snakes were on the table, waiting to be packed.

Pickles the cat was watching from the armchair, her tail curled around her like a comma.

'Look at you, Rosie,' said Molly. She gave her a hug. 'You look fantastic.'

Rosie was now dressed as a mermaid princess. Her mum had made the costume – a shiny purple bikini top and a sparkly green tail. Her brown hair was topped with a silver diamante tiara and her arms were laden with silver bangles.

'Thanks, Molly,' replied Rosie, with a big smile. 'I'm still doing the lolly bags.'

Lulu sighed and crossed her arms impatiently.

'Rosie, you should have finished the drawings by now. It's time to pack the lolly bags.'

Rosie looked at the small pile of finished drawings. She had decorated each one with mermaids, fish, shells, underwater creatures and coral. There were still six to do.

Rosie's brow wrinkled and her

mouth turned down. 'They're taking a long time,' she agreed.

Lulu picked up one of the drawings.

'Well, they *are* really pretty,' she said. 'Don't worry. Molly and I will get dressed and then we'll help you. Three of us will get it done much faster.'

Lulu checked on the morning's cooking. The beautiful mermaid cake was on the bench. The square brownie tin was cooling on a high shelf, out of Gus's reach. Lulu opened the fridge and shook one of the jellies.

'We still have to decorate the jelly cups with green snakes,' she said.

'And set up the games,' added Molly. 'But there's plenty of time.'

Lulu thought hard. *What party games would make Rosie's party* really *special?*

Chapter 5

Disaster

In the girls' bedroom, Lulu and Molly
changed out of their T-shirts and leggings.
They put on the costumes that Mum had
made for them. Lulu had a blue top and
green tail, while Molly had a silver top
and blue tail. Lulu looked at herself in
the mirror. She didn't look anything like
her usual self, except for her long honey-
coloured plaits.

The sparkly material swished around

Lulu's legs. 'It's a little hard to walk in a tail,' she joked. 'Give me leggings any day.'

'Yes, but it is fun to dress up,' said Molly. 'I like being a mermaid.'

Molly twirled in front of the mirror.

'Your mum is so clever,' she said. 'And that cake is so cool. I'm so glad she asked us to help with the party.'

'She is creative,' said Lulu proudly, 'but I guess artists have to be.'

'You are creative too, Lulu,' replied Molly. 'You have the most wonderful ideas!'

Lulu felt a thrill of pleasure at Molly's praise. She smiled at her friend.

'Come on,' said Lulu. 'Let's get those games organised.'

As Lulu came down the hall, she heard a funny noise coming from the kitchen. It was a thumping, sliding, bumping sound.

Mum was at the front door. She was hanging green paper streamers to make a curtain of

39

seaweed. Rosie was handing her pieces of sticky tape. Big silver fish made of foil had been stuck along the walls. Mum had also painted two beautiful mermaids on butcher's paper. They stood guard on either side of the front door.

Suddenly a loud crash came from the kitchen.

'Gus?' called Lulu. 'Are you all right?'

There was no reply. Then Asha woofed – a loud warning bark.

Lulu began to run. She threw open the door and gasped. A dreadful sight greeted her.

The back door was wide open. The little white pony stood in the middle of the kitchen. He had his head down and was nudging something around the floor. Something green and blue and silver. Something smashed and shattered that he was gobbling with glee. Asha stood on guard behind him, her ears pricked and hackles raised.

'The cake!' shouted Lulu in horror.

Molly ran. Mum ran. Rosie ran. They stood in the doorway and stared at the terrible mess. Gus came from the garden to the back door and peered in. Jessie followed at his heels.

'Horsie ate the cake,' announced Gus. He popped his grubby thumb in his mouth.

The pony kept eating, smearing the cake into the floorboards.

Rosie burst into tears. 'My cake. My beautiful mermaid cake.'

The pony looked up innocently. Cake crumbs and green icing were smudged over his lips and whiskers. His brown eyes were large and soft.

He whinnied and dropped his head to keep guzzling.

Mum rubbed her forehead as she

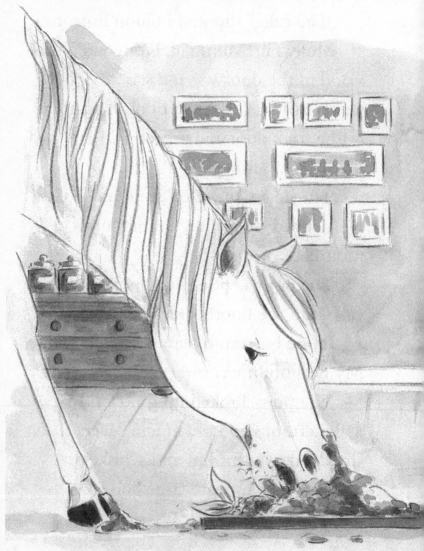

surveyed the wreck of her hours of work.
She kissed Rosie on top of her head and
hugged her close.

'I'm so sorry, Rosie,' said Mum. 'That
cake is definitely beyond saving.'

Rosie sobbed and hiccupped.

Lulu had a terrible thought. She glared at Gus.

'Gus, did you let the pony into the kitchen?' she demanded.

Gus tried to change the subject. 'I not Gus, I Bug Boy?' he said hopefully.

'Come on, girls,' said Mum with a sigh. 'Let's get that pony outside and clean up this mess. Rosie's friends will be here soon.'

'It's all right, Rosie,' said Lulu. She patted her sister on the shoulder. 'We'll think of something.'

Lulu grabbed Jessie's lead from the cupboard. Then she caught the pony's halter. She led him out of the kitchen and into the garden. The pony looked at her sadly. He reminded Lulu of a picture in one of Rosie's favourite fairytale

books. Lulu gently pulled a twig from his mane and wiped the icing from his whiskers.

'Oh, you naughty pony,' whispered Lulu. 'You've ruined Rosie's party.'

The pony whickered and blew warm air on Lulu's cheek. She stroked his neck.

'But I can't scold you. You're too beautiful.'

Chapter 6

Another Plan

Back inside, Mum was on her hands and knees. She was sweeping up the shattered

cake with the dustpan and brush. Gus was hiding under the kitchen table with his arm around Asha's neck. He had his thumb in his mouth and looked rather guilty. Jessie thumped her tail on the floorboards and smiled at Lulu.

Molly was helping Rosie to finish drawing on the lolly bags. Rosie dropped her pencil in despair, then she sniffed and wiped her eyes.

'Cheer up, Rosie,' said Molly. She gave the younger girl a hug. 'It will still be a lovely party.'

Lulu flicked one of her plaits over her shoulder and looked about the room. She went to the sink and fetched a cloth. Then she dropped down beside her mum and helped wipe up the sticky icing smears.

'Careful of your tail, honey bun,' warned Mum. 'We don't want that covered in cake too.'

Lulu smiled at her mother and hitched her tail out of the way.

'What will we do about a birthday cake?' Lulu whispered. 'We can't have a birthday party without a cake.'

Her mum shrugged. She pushed her hair out of her eyes and smeared icing on her cheek. She checked the kitchen clock.

'The local bakery shuts at two o'clock on Saturdays, so we can't get a cake there,' said Mum. She tipped the dustpan of lolly shards and cake crumbs into the bin. 'Perhaps I could get something at the supermarket?'

'But it wouldn't be a mermaid cake,' said Lulu. 'It wouldn't suit Rosie's theme.'

Lulu thought carefully while she wiped the floor. *A cake. A cake . . . How can we make a special cake for Rosie?*

Chapter 7

Lulu to the Rescue

Lulu ran to the bedroom she shared with Rosie. Pepper, the ginger cat, was curled up on her bed. The cat yawned and stretched in greeting.

In the corner of the room was a big wooden castle. It was crowded with toy knights, princesses, elves and animals. Lulu searched the figures carefully. She picked out a handful and ran back to the kitchen.

'Mum, Mum,' called Lulu. 'I have an idea for the cake.'

Mum was mopping the floor. Rosie and Molly stopped stuffing lollies into bags and looked up. Gus crawled out from under the table and pushed back his Bug Boy mask. Jessie pricked up her ears.

Lulu set out the figures on the kitchen bench. She had chosen an elf princess and elf prince, a tree and a white unicorn with a golden horn.

'What if we iced the brownie cake? Then we could decorate it with the elves and the unicorn. We could put the blue jelly all around the base to make a sea. Then Rosie could draw some mermaids and we could cut them out and make them swim in the sea.'

Mum stood the mop in the corner.

She glanced at the clock. Rosie looked at her hopefully.

'We only have half an hour,' said Mum. 'We'd have to work fast ...'

She took the cooled chocolate brownie cake down from the shelf.

'*Mmmmm.*' Mum smiled at Lulu. 'Brilliant idea, honey bun. Okay – I'll make the icing and you girls get to work on some mermaids.'

Mum started mixing up a new batch of icing. Gus stood beside her on a stool. He helped by sticking a teaspoon in the icing mixture, stirring, and then licking the spoon. Jessie helped by waiting beside the bench in case any crumbs fell and needed to be cleaned up.

Molly and Rosie went back to work at the kitchen table. They finished the lolly bags and began to sketch mermaids on white paper. Lulu went to the craft cupboard. She pulled out some cardboard, scissors, the stapler, a purple ribbon and some paint. She checked to make sure nobody was watching her. Then she crept off to her bedroom to work on a secret project.

'We've got twenty minutes,' called Mum. 'We'll have to go faster.'

A little while later, Lulu came back to the kitchen. The cake was now iced a pale shade of green. Gus was sitting on the floor. His mask was pulled back and his face was in the mixing bowl. His Bug Boy suit was speckled with chocolate and icing. Jessie tried to clean him up by licking the goo from his clothes.

Mum was cutting up jelly snakes. She pressed the pieces into flower shapes around the edge of the cake. She had already chopped out small fish shapes.

'I'll get the jelly and start spooning out the sea,' offered Lulu. She scooped out the blue jelly. Then she arranged it around the base of the cake to form waves and ripples.

'Ten minutes,' warned Mum. She scattered golden fish on the jelly sea.

Lulu helped Molly and Rosie to cut out the paper mermaids. Gus helped by licking out the empty jelly cups.

'Five minutes to go . . .' cried Mum. She placed the unicorn under the tree on top of the cake. 'And it's finished!'

Everyone crowded around.

'It's fantastic,' said Molly. 'Take some more photos.'

'Is *'dorable*,' declared Gus, his face smeared blue and green.

'I love it,' sighed Rosie. Her face was shining with relief. 'You're so clever, Mum – and you too, Lulu. It was a really good idea.'

Lulu felt a warm glow spread through her body. She looked up at her mum. Mum looked tired. She had a new stripe of green icing across her cheek and speckles on her shirt. Lulu picked up a damp tea towel and climbed up on the stool. She gently wiped the icing from her mother's cheek.

'Now it's time for you to get ready, Mum,' urged Lulu. 'You're the only one not dressed up.'

Mum
kissed Lulu on
the forehead.
'Thanks,
honey bun,' said
Mum. 'You've been
a great help.'

Lulu smiled with happiness.

'Come on, Molly,' said Lulu. 'We've still got to set up the games in the garden. Rosie, you stay in here with Gus. The games have to be a surprise.'

Chapter 8

A Mob of Mermaids

The front doorbell rang and Rosie's friends began to arrive. The girls were all dressed as mermaids. They wore long fishy tails and jewels in their hair. They carried mysterious coloured packages under their arms.

The girls giggled as they ducked under the seaweed curtain. They *oohed* and *aahed* when they saw that the hall was swimming with silvery fish.

Mum waved her wand in greeting.
She was dressed as a regal fairy princess.
She wore a long velvet cloak over her
sparkly dress and a tiara on her head.

'Welcome to the underwater
kingdom of Princess Rosie the Mermaid,'
cried Mum. 'Please place your kind
offerings on the
kitchen table for
the princess to
peruse at her
pleasure.'

Rosie giggled with excitement as she greeted her friends.

'Hi, Mia. Hi, Gracie. Hello, Ruby ... come in ... come in.'

'Happy birthday, Rosie,' called Ruby. 'You look so pretty.'

The girls crowded into the kitchen.

61

They admired each other's outfits and compared the size and shapes of the presents on the table. Pickles took one look at all the guests and stalked away to find a quiet place to sleep.

Jessie bounded over to welcome all the mermaids. She smiled broadly and wagged her tail wildly. Rosie had dressed the dog in a pink tutu and wings. The wings had slipped off to one side.

Gus crawled out from under the table. He was still dressed in his Bug Boy suit but Lulu had wiped his face clean.

One of the mothers smiled at Gus. 'Hello, who's this little mermaid?' she asked.

'I not mermaid,' declared Gus in disgust. 'I Bug Boy!'

'Yes, you are Bug Boy, honey bun,' replied Mum. She kissed the top of his masked head. 'And you're adorable.'

'I not . . .' began Gus.

Lulu grabbed him by the hand and dragged him towards the door.

'Come on, Gussie,' she said. 'Let's show Rosie her birthday surprise.'

Chapter 9
The Underwater Kingdom

Lulu threw open the door and everyone crowded around. The garden had been transformed into an underwater pleasure ground. Balloons and coloured lanterns and seaweed streamers were strung in the trees.

Silken cushions were scattered on a blue tarpaulin 'sea' and soft music played.

A mermaid piñata hung from a broad branch and the shallow paddle pool was filled with fragrant bubbles.

And best of all, in the very centre was a unicorn. His white coat had been brushed until it shone. His mane and tail rippled like silk in the sunlight. In the centre of his forehead was a golden horn tied with purple ribbon.

'A unicorn,' shrieked Rosie. 'You've turned the pony into a unicorn!'

Lulu winked at her sister. Molly laughed in delight.

'Who'd like a unicorn ride?' cried Lulu, flicking a plait over her shoulder. 'Who will ride upon Stardust, the noble unicorn steed?'

The little mermaids clamoured around Lulu. 'Me! Me!' they squealed.

'Princess Rosie, the birthday girl!

You shall have the honour of the very first ride upon Stardust the unicorn,' pronounced Lulu.

She led the way into the underwater garden.

First Rosie, then all the other mermaid friends rode around and around

the garden. Lulu led the pony.

'Stardust the unicorn' behaved beautifully. He didn't go near the unicorn cake – but he did take a bite from the pink daisy bush on his way past.

After the rides, the girls had their faces painted by Lulu and Molly.

Then they searched for hidden treasure
and chocolate eggs in the flowerbeds.
They cuddled Flopsy, the pet rabbit,
played musical cushions on the tarpaulin
sea and danced like mermaids. There was
a pass-the-parcel and smash-the-piñata
and splashing races through the bubble
pool.

Lulu laughed as she joined in. So far,
the party was a success!

Chapter 10

Serena and Snowy

Dr Bell arrived at the side gate. The girls were throwing handfuls of bubbles at each other and screaming with glee. Behind him came a woman and a girl. The girl was dressed in jodhpurs and riding boots. Her dark hair was tied back in two plaits, just like Lulu's. The girl looked pale and red-eyed, as though she had been crying.

'Snowy!' she shrieked. She ran and

threw her arms around the unicorn's neck. She buried her face in his mane.

'This is Mrs Winters, and this is her daughter Serena,' introduced Dr Bell. 'As you might have guessed, Snowy the pony belongs to them. Mrs Winters, this is my wife Chrissie, and my daughters Lulu and Rosie. All the other mermaids are her friends.'

Mum came over to say hello.

'I can't thank you enough, Dr
Bell,' said Mrs Winters. 'We've been so
worried. Snowy was missing from his
paddock this morning when Serena went
to feed him. We think somebody let him
out deliberately. The gate was closed last
night.'

Mum shook her head in dismay.

'Who would do such a dreadful
thing?' she said. 'Snowy could have been
killed on the road or broken a leg.'

'Poor Serena has been so upset,' Mrs
Winters whispered. 'She's been crying
all morning. We rang the police, the fire
department, the radio station – everyone
we could think of. We were so relieved
when the police rang to say that Dr Bell
had found Snowy.'

Lulu went over to Serena and Snowy.

Serena looked up from Snowy's neck and smiled a watery smile.

'Hi, Serena – I'm Lulu.'

'Thanks for rescuing Snowy,' said Serena. 'Did you make the unicorn costume?'

'Yes,' said Lulu. 'I dressed Snowy as a unicorn to cheer Rosie up. You see, it's her birthday and Snowy did the wickedest thing. Well, actually, it was

probably my brother Gus's fault, but he's only three.'

Lulu told Serena the whole story. Serena laughed at the thought of Snowy stealing the cake and having his whiskers covered in green icing.

'I guess it *is* funny,' admitted Lulu. 'But it wasn't at the time.'

'Well, Snowy definitely makes a beautiful unicorn,' said Serena. She stroked his forelock and straightened his horn. Then she looked back at Lulu. 'You can come and visit Snowy at our place. Any time you'd like.'

'Do you mean it?' asked Lulu. Her eyes were shining with excitement. 'I'd love to.'

'We could go riding together,' added Serena. 'We have a big paddock at home that backs onto the bush trails. I go riding nearly every afternoon after school.'

Lulu grinned at Serena. 'That would be awesome.'

Mum called the girls over.

'Rosie, Lulu. Mrs Winters has brought you something. She wants to say happy birthday and thank you for rescuing Snowy.'

Mrs Winters had brought in a large box from her car. It was wrapped in white paper and tied with a giant green ribbon.

'When I rang the vet hospital, the nurse told me that you were celebrating Rosie's birthday. So I thought we should bring something along,' explained Mrs Winters.

'Help me open it, Lulu?' asked Rosie. 'It's heavy!'

Together they undid the ribbon and

tore open the paper.

Inside the box was a pile of lovely books.
Beautiful picture books with gorgeous
illustrations. Thick chapter books with
enticing covers. Adventure books and
fairytales and all kinds of exciting books
in between.

Rosie shrieked with excitement.

'Serena helped me choose them,'
explained Mrs Winters. 'I hope you like
them.'

'Thank you, Mrs Winters,' cried Lulu and Rosie together. They *oohed* and *aahed* as they flicked through the pages and read the back covers.

'We'll have to keep these away from Gus,' Lulu warned Rosie. Gus scowled and stuck his thumb in his mouth. 'But I'll read them to you, Gus, I promise.'

A buzzer went off in the kitchen.

'Oh, the sausage rolls,' cried Mum. 'I nearly forgot. Would you and Serena like to stay for the mermaid feast, Mrs Winters? I'm just about to serve it.'

Serena looked hopefully at her mother. Snowy cropped the grass, his tail swishing with contentment. His horn had slipped back over one ear.

'I'll help you load Snowy in my trailer after the feast,' offered Dr Bell. 'Then I can run him home for you.'

'That would be wonderful,' replied Mrs Winters. 'Thank you, Mrs Bell, we'd love to stay.'

'Thanks, Mum,' cried Serena. 'Thanks, Mrs Bell.'

Chapter 11

The Mermaid Feast

Lulu and Molly helped to lay the food out on the feast table. There were steaming sausage rolls and tomato sauce, tiny party pies and, of course, fish bites. A blue platter held sea-grapes, strawberries and sea-watermelon. Another held mermaid-bread topped with blue and green sprinkles.

All the mermaids came to sit around the table. Rosie sat at the head,

on a throne draped in purple velvet.

Gus sat at the other end with his
mask still covering half his face. He had
two bowls right in front of him. One
overflowed with crunchy chocolate
crackles. The other held crispy, salty chips.

Jessie and Asha sat on either side of
him. Their heads followed the movement
of Gus's hand from bowl to mouth and
back again.

Gus stuffed two chocolate crackles in his mouth. *'Mmmm. Dulishus.'*

'Oh, no you don't, Gussie,' said Lulu. She rescued the bowl of chocolate crackles before they all disappeared.

Lulu, Serena and Molly sat down next to Gus to share in the feast.

'You're right, Gus,' said Molly. 'These chocolate crackles are really good.'

Suddenly Mum jumped up and ran inside. She came back with a mysterious bulging bag.

'I nearly forgot,' confessed Mum. Her eyes twinkled with mischief. 'Here are your royal robes, King Neptune.'

'Oh, no,' groaned Dad. He stepped backwards with his hands raised. 'I'm not dressing up.'

'Come on, Dad,' called Lulu and Rosie together.

'*Please,*' Rosie added, jiggling up and down.

Dad looked around at all the mermaids. He rolled his eyes in mock horror and sighed. 'Well, all right.'

'Here you are, Your Highness,' offered Mum.

She pulled a white sheet over his shoulder and fastened it with a safety pin. Then she slipped a long blue cloak around his neck. She had made a white wig and beard from wispy cotton wool. This was topped with a gold cardboard crown.

Last of all, Mum handed him a golden trident made from an old broomstick.

'Let the feast begin,' thundered King Neptune. He flourished his trident.

Lulu and Rosie giggled with delight. Mum snapped photographs of King

Neptune and Princess Rosie and all the girls in their sparkly costumes.

The girls chattered and laughed and ate. Mum served plastic goblets filled with blue lemonade, with orange 'fish' bobbing in the bubbles.

'Mmmmm – *melonade*,' said Gus. 'Bug Boy like *melonade*.'

Then Mum carried out the unicorn cake. The jelly sea wobbled and joggled, making the paper mermaids dance. The candles flared and sputtered. Everyone sang 'Happy Birthday' to Rosie.

The tiny unicorn stood proudly on top of the cake. In the garden, Snowy whinnied loudly.

'Blow out the candles and make a wish, honey bun,' said Mum.

Rosie closed her eyes. She took a big deep breath and blew. The candles

flickered and fizzled. Mum cut up the
cake and put a piece in each bowl. Lulu
added wobbly blue jelly and vanilla
ice-cream.

'What did you wish for?' asked Molly.

'I can't tell you or it won't come true,'
replied Rosie.

She beamed around the table at all

her friends. Then she looked up at her parents.

'Thanks, Mum. Thanks, Dad. Thanks for all your help, Molly.'

Then she turned and smiled an extra-big grin at her sister.

'Thanks for finding me a birthday unicorn, Lulu,' Rosie said. 'This has been the best birthday party ever!'

Lulu grinned back. She flicked one of her plaits over her shoulder.

'It was a pleasure, Rosie. Maybe we can get our own snow-white pony to keep in the backyard?'

She looked up hopefully at her parents.

'No!' cried Mum and Rosie and Molly together.

Dad rubbed his chin, then winked at Lulu.

'Mmmm,' he said. 'Maybe.'

Lulu and her dad exchanged a secret smile.

'Fantabulous!' said Lulu.

Illustrated by Serena Geddes

BELINDA MURRELL

Lulu Bell

and the
Fairy Penguin

Lulu Bell and the Fairy Penguin

It's a hot day and the Bell family is going for a swim. But when a runaway dog chases a little penguin that is waddling up the beach, Lulu has to leap into action!

Is the little penguin hurt? And as if that's not enough for Lulu to worry about, where is Pickles the cat, who's about to have her kittens? Let the search begin!

Out now

Read all the Lulu Bell books